The Legend of the Twenty-first North Pole Santa

By

Denise Graham Zahn

© 2001, 2002 by Denise Graham Zahn. All rights reserved.

No part of this book may be reproduced, stored in a retrieval system, or transmitted by any means, electronic, mechanical, photocopying, recording, or otherwise, without written permission from the author.

ISBN: 1-4033-4800-6 (Electronic)
ISBN: 1-4033-4801-4 (Softcover)
ISBN: 1-4033-4802-2 (Dustjacket)

Library of Congress Control Number: 2002092859

This book is printed on acid free paper.

Printed in the United States of America
Bloomington, IN

Illustrated by Tad and Dana Graham

1stBooks – rev. 08/28/02

Dedicated

To all the Believers of the World who thought the magic of Santa Claus was over. The magic didn't end when you couldn't believe that he could deliver presents to Believing Children all over the world. The story was simply incomplete.

Read "The Legend of the Twenty-First North Pole Santa" and Believe again.

And if you are so inclined, pass it on.

The author

Table of Contents

Chapter I	A Fine Pair	1
Chapter II	Little Star	5
Chapter III	Disappointment	9
Chapter IV	The Weather	19
Chapter V	Cousin Nicky	23
Chapter VI	The Elf Story	29
Chapter VII	The Weather Worsens	41
Chapter VIII	Santa Family Pow Wow	53
Chapter IX	Show Time	59
Chapter X	On to Anchorage	71
Chapter XI	Rudy	81
Chapter XII	We're Back!	89
Chapter XIII	Return Trip	97
Chapter XIV	Christmas is Over	103
Epilogue		107

# Chapter I A Fine Pair

Denise Graham Zahn

"I'm so excited, Rudy," said Holly. "Everyone will arrive by tomorrow night, as long as the weather holds out. Papa said we're supposed to get some really bad weather soon, though. I hope it doesn't cause problems at the airport for incoming flights. At least if they get here, I know you and the other Magic Reindeer will certainly get them out on time."

She stopped brushing Rudy's coat for a moment and looked at the animal contentedly munching his hay. He turned his aged but bright brown eyes toward her, still munching, and Holly switched her focus to him. That was Holly's nature, to be concerned about others, and that's why she was so special to everyone, including this old red-nosed reindeer.

"You must be getting excited, too, Rudy," she said. "Christmas is your time to shine, as everybody knows!" Rudy was Holly's favorite among the reindeer, though she didn't let on to the others. But Rudy knew and enjoyed his favored position in Holly's generous heart.

Resuming where she left off in brushing his coat, Holly continued her one-sided conversation. After giving a short snort and a shrug of his head, Rudy turned his head back and continued to savor his meal and Holly's company.

"This year is going to be a special Christmas for me," Holly said. "Once everyone arrives and my cousins and I are initiated to take the Christmas reins, I will officially be installed as the next North Pole Santa – the twenty-first generation of North Pole Santas. I'll follow in Papa's footsteps just as he followed in his Papa's and his Papa's before him – clear back to the first North Pole Santa, who was called Chris Kringle, Father Christmas and St. Nicholas. It's a fine heritage, Rudy, and you and I will be together forever."

Herald Santa Claus, Holly's Papa, was just coming into the stable to talk to Holly when he picked up the last part of her conversation. He sighed heavily. He loved his daughter as deeply as any father had ever loved a child, and he was about to break her heart — and no father should ever have to break his child's heart.

Chapter II Little Star

Denise Graham Zahn

Papa stood for a moment watching Holly, remembering her as an infant and then a toddler. Holly was the most beautiful of babies, with lots of black gleaming hair and a round rosy face. She always had a twinkle, Papa said, right from the time she was born. That's why Papa called her his little star. He smiled for an instant, remembering this and how it delighted Holly to be called "Little Star." Then his thoughts turned to a time some 13 years ago.

Papa's wife, Merry, had been caretaker for a dozen or more children in North Pole. These were the children of locals who knew that Merry would care for their children with the loving tenderness they themselves provided. They were Athabascan, Inuit, American Indian and non-native Alaskans whose families had moved there from the American mainland. The children were a joy to Merry, who sadly found that she and Papa could never have children of their own. These children kept her busy and Papa was as happy as she to have them around.

That winter was brutally cold, and the snow just never seemed to stop. The accumulation was deeper than anyone remembered. A blizzard had just started when the parents were arriving to pick up their children from Merry. All the parents arrived except for the parents of one little girl. Papa and Merry were concerned when they didn't arrive within half an hour of the other parents and called the local police to begin a search. The news was not good.

On that day the child became an orphan with no family to take her in, unusual in this community. It was a clear message to Merry, however, that this child should be hers and Papa's. So Holly, the little star, child of Athabascan parents, that Papa and Merry had cared for since birth, became their adopted child, and they would be the only parents that "Little Star" would remember, though Papa and Merry paid careful attention to honor Holly's birth parents, as well as her Athabascan heritage.

The adoption, however, raised more than a few eyebrows in the Santa Claus family.

Chapter III Disappointment

Denise Graham Zahn

Papa snapped out of his reverie when he heard Holly begin to whistle a Christmas song to Rudy. Of course it was the one she thought was Rudy's favorite – "Rudolph the Red-Nosed Reindeer." Papa had never regretted for one instant their decision to make Holly his daughter and only child. But he knew that day would come when a decision would be made, and the decision was not his alone to make.

"Hey, Little Star, Rudy's looking mighty good. You sure he's not your favorite? Are you going to make the others look this good for the Christmas season?"

"Oh, Papa, you know I will," Holly laughed. Just as quickly as he had smiled Papa stopped smiling. Holly was as connected to her father as if his blood truly ran through her veins. As he approached her she felt a sadness in him that she had only occasionally felt before. He would always brush it off, but something was different this time. He didn't even try to say something silly to wave it off as he usually did. For a moment, she thought he was ill or that Mama was – and it scared her. "Papa, are you ill?" Little Star asked. "Is Mama sick?"

"No, no, Little Star. I'm fine and so is Mama. It's you I'm worried about," he said. "Why Papa," she asked. It's almost Christmas, everyone will be arriving soon, and I will have my official appointment. This is a wonderful time for me, and I love seeing my cousins. We have so much fun."

Papa's mood did not change. Softly he said, "Listen, child," and directed her to sit on a bale of straw beside him. "You know Mama and I love you and feel blessed to have you in our lives, and have always honored your birth parents and your cultural heritage. You also know that my brothers, nephews and many cousins and distant cousins love you. But, Little Star, you are the first girl in the Santa Claus family. No Santa Claus has ever produced a girl, and my brothers have decided that only the first naturally born son of the North Pole Santa should receive this birthright."

Now she understood. For the first time in her entire life, Holly was shaken. Her rosy cheeks paled. Her smile disappeared. Rudolph felt the change and bellowed out the pain that Holly felt. She walked over and placed her arm around his neck, as though it were Rudolph that needed comforting.

So this was the sadness that Papa never spoke of, she thought — that Holly would never be accepted as North Pole Santa – by her own family. Papa took a deep breath and continued talking for fear that he wouldn't be able to get it out at all if it didn't tumble out all at once. "You, Little Star," he said, "don't qualify under those rules. Therefore, they have decided by majority rule, that the birthright should be passed to the first naturally born son of the next in line – my brother Noel's first son Nickolai." Holly called him Nicky.

Closing his eyes slowly in an effort to keep composed, Papa opened them again to complete the blow. He was struggling to keep the tears from tumbling, his voice from breaking. "To make matters worse, Little Star, they have voted not to allow you rights to run a Christmas sleigh."

As he finished those last words the twinkle left Little Star's eyes. Papa could almost see them flickering out. He didn't know where it went. He just knew that it was gone. All the love he and Mama had for her couldn't fix this. What Herald Santa Claus, the Twentieth North Pole Santa wasn't aware of, was that his own twinkle was gone. Again, it was as if his blood coursed through Holly's veins as sure as if she were his own natural child – and when her twinkle left – his glow turned off – like a switch that had been flicked or a fuse that had been blown.

Holly's birthright had been taken again. She'd been robbed of her first birthright when her parents died. Now she was being robbed because she was a girl and because she was Athabascan, not naturally born to North Pole Santa and his wife. Papa was sick. He knew there was little he could do. While his vote weighed heavier than that of his brothers individually, he could not oppose them all, and he knew that his brother Noel was dead set against Holly inheriting not only the North Pole Santa position, but of becoming an official Santa at all.

"Holly," Papa said, "You know the traditions as well as I do. It is tradition that all firsts are family decisions — just as it had been a family decision, for instance, that only one Santa remained in the Arctic region as North Pole Santa for each generation." Papa was rambling, looking for something that would make the hurt go away – for both him and Holly.

"Originally, remember, there was only one Santa Claus in the entire world. The very first North Pole Santa and his wife had six boys, and as they came of age they delivered gifts to children in a growing world population." Holly knew the story, but she never minded hearing it again, knowing that one day she would become not only a Santa but a North Pole Santa. Right now, though, hearing the story was different. She knew Papa needed to talk, so she listened.

Papa went on, "At a time when the boys became men, which is at the initiation, you know, the family decided that each son should live on a different continent, with the oldest son remaining at the North Pole. The sons each took a wife from the country where they made their home, and the Santa Claus family increased right along with the size of the Believing World." Holly heard the pride in Papa's voice as he said, "That's why today there are Santas of every race and ethnic background all around the world." A few minutes passed before Papa spoke again. Holly could see his shoulders rise and fall in a silent sigh. But shortly he picked up where he had left off.

"It was also a family decision, Holly, that at the passing of each North Pole Santa his oldest son would inherit the North Pole Santa position, so that he would be the second generation North Pole Santa, then the third North Pole Santa, and so on. Of course," he added, "As you know, Santas live an extraordinarily long time, but they do eventually grow old and pass on just as Magic Reindeer do. The Magic Reindeer, of course, live even longer than Santas but not forever, either."

Papa turned to see Holly's reaction. She always loved Papa's stories, but she was quiet today, though still listening intently. Understanding her mood, Papa brought the story to an end. "These were all family decisions, Holly." But, Papa thought, those decisions were not hurtful, and were unanimous decisions reached by all the brothers.

This was different. It seemed to him that as his family spread out across the world, they had become hardened and distant in spirit. They had lost the spirit of North Pole Santa and Christmas. Holly was the Twentieth North Pole Santa's child. Being an adopted girl didn't change that. In fact, Papa thought, it only added to the spirit of the Christmas season. It was a sad, sad day for Papa, Mama, Holly – and the world.

It was Holly that brought Papa back to the moment at hand. She knew he felt very badly, just as she did, and just as she was sure

Mama did. But Holly told her Papa, "I'm alright, Papa. I can be strong. I have you and Mama and a strong and proud Athabascan heritage, as well." Holly held her father's hand and comforted him.

"Let's go in," she said. "I'm sure Mama's fixing something wonderful for our guests, and I want to be the first to taste it." The words were right, but they rang hollow to Papa. Nonetheless, he followed his daughter in, leaving Rudy and the other Magic Reindeer to their dinner.

Rudy's eyes glistened, as a small tear fell at the corner of his eye. Once more, he let out a groan, and Holly reached out and gently lifted his chin, giving her friend a small sign of her deep affection to comfort him.

Denise Graham Zahn

Chapter IV The Weather

Denise Graham Zahn

The Legend of the Twenty-First North Pole Santa

The weather was getting worse. Just like that fateful day so many years before, when Holly lost her parents, the snow just didn't stop, very unusual for an area that was usually cold but dry. And the wind was ferocious. The weather was getting bad enough, in fact, the Fairbanks Airport, the airport closest to North Pole, was considering shutting down. And though many Santas and their families had already arrived and had checked into rooms in North Pole, many others had not. Still, Holly wasn't worried.

Christmas Eve was a day away and this time of year was always full of celebration and storytelling for the family, locals and many visiting Believers. These days just before Christmas were always the best for Holly.

Along with all the stories that she'd heard over and over but never enough, she loved playing with her cousins, all boys, but nonetheless, her family. They didn't care that she was a girl – and not one said or even thought that being adopted made Holly any less a cousin than they were to each other.

Because past generations had gone off to live in the many Believing Countries on the various continents, each of her cousins had a dramatically different appearance. Some were Asian, some African, some European. Some were chubby and some were slim. Some had dark complexions with dark hair, while others had fair complexions and fair hair. Others still, had fair complexions with dark hair. Some had curly hair, others straight. Some were tall, while others were short. Some had green eyes or blue eyes, while others had brown eyes and any combination of those.

Each of her cousins had a unique personality and represented the customs and costume of their background. But through it ran a common thread. They were family, and Holly alone was not born to the family but chosen to be part of it. "Now is not the time to think about this," Holly said silently. "Today I'm going to have fun." And for the moment, she forgot about her own situation and became lost in the commotion of the holiday.

Chapter V   Cousin Nicky

Denise Graham Zahn

Holly was anxious to see her favorite cousin, Nickolai, Nicky as she called him. He was Uncle Noel's older of two sons, and Uncle Noel was the oldest of all Papa's eleven younger brothers. Uncle Noel and his family lived in Russia, and while her Uncle Noel spoke English like Papa and all the brothers, Nicky spoke English with a Russian accent, just as many of her first cousins spoke English flavored with the accent of their native country. Holly just loved listening to them, but mostly she just loved Nicky.

Holly was in her home, already getting crowded with uncles, aunts, cousins and neighbors. Everywhere the topic was the same – how bad the weather was getting. Just as Holly entered the great room where a painting of the first North Pole Santa hung, she saw Nicky and he saw her. She also saw Uncle Noel looking at her.

She instantly saw the tension in their faces. Uncle Noel turned away, but Nicky came towards her. "Nicky," Holly cried out. "Oh, Nicky! I'm so glad you are here." Upon hearing that, Nicky's face lost all tension and turned to joy. "Holly, Little Star, you have grown so much since last year. Just look at you," he blurted out with admiration.

"Look at you, Nicky. How did you get so big in just one year – and so handsome besides?" Nicky laughed as he grabbed both of Holly's hands and swung her around in a sort of "Ring Around the Rosies" formation, despite the crowd. "Oh, Nicky, stop!" she laughed. "I can't get used to your transformation. Why you almost look like Papa with your white whiskers and hair, and it's only been four years since your initiation."

"Ho! Ho! Ho!" Nicky laughed, and Holly noted that it was a deep laugh, one that came straight from his heart. Then their eyes met, and she knew her 20-year old cousin wanted to say something that was not a laughing matter. He edged her toward an open space in the crowded room.

Holly quickly said to herself. "I will not let this come between Nicky and me. He is too special." Nicky felt the same way and knew that he had to say something to Holly about the decision. "Holly," he said slowly, "It was not my decision. I had no part in it and would not have chosen it. You know very well, Holly, that you are no different than any of our cousins." Then he grinned a little and said quietly, pretending it was a secret, "Except that you are my favorite, that is."

The Legend of the Twenty-First North Pole Santa

Holly smiled back, knowing that Nicky knew he had always been her favorite, ever since she became a part of the family.

After a slight pause, Nicky continued, while Holly adjusted her listening to the accent she hadn't heard since last year. "Holly I know your birthright, and I know you are entitled to it. I have no desire to take it from you, but I can't go against the decision of the brothers as a whole."

Again he paused and took a deep breath before continuing. "I know that it is my father that started the wheels turning in this direction. He was also responsible for convincing the majority of the brothers that the birthright extended only to natural born sons. I don't know why he is so stubborn on this, Holly. I know he loves you."

That was it. Nicky had said what he had to say and could say no more than that. He could not change anything. He could only tell Holly how he felt.

Now it was Holly's turn to speak. "Nicky," she said, "It is hard. I know you know that. Papa is heartbroken and believes he has let me down. I love you all, though, so I simply cannot think about it now. I just have to believe that something will work out in the end. It just has to."

After a momentary pause, Holly's enthusiasm for the season and love for her cousin restored her spirits and she abruptly stated, "So let's not talk about that now. I want to hear the stories, and they are going to start soon. The elf story is first and Papa is the very best storyteller."

Nicky laughed a hearty heartfelt laugh, swung Holly around by the hands one more time. "You are truly Little Star," he said. "You brighten even a sky like today's, and I am sorry, Little Star, that because of me you have lost your birthright to be not only the next North Pole Santa but to be initiated to run the Christmas sleighs."

Chapter VI   The Elf Story

Denise Graham Zahn

It was December 23rd, and that was the night when the official storytelling began. Holly was excited. She couldn't help it. It was an overwhelming experience every year. The storytelling brought in folks from the entire region of the North Pole – and some who flew in from as far away as Russia, China, Australia and Florida and New York on the U.S. mainland.

These were people who wanted to hear the stories of the season and to celebrate giving. They wanted to participate in something extraordinary and to instill the concept of the joy of giving in their children. This was a time of touching and reaching out and listening – and it was fun!

"Look at everyone, Nicky. They are all laughing and smiling, just the way it should be." "You're right, Little Star," he replied, "but there is some concern about the weather. While some of the Santas and their families have arrived, most have not. I know it always snows this time of year, but a blizzard has been brewing all day, and predictions are that it will get worse over the next few days."

Holly looked around and could see people occasionally glancing out the windows before turning to talk again. Still, spirits were high, and there was not yet a great deal of concern. "But, Nicky," Holly assured her cousin, "There has never been a cancellation of the Christmas celebration not even during the terrible fog when Rudy joined the sleigh team eons ago." Nicky laughed again, "You're right as always, Holly. Now let's listen to your Papa's wonderful storytelling."

They left the great room, which is where people were busy talking and eating and went into the large sitting room, where the fireplace was blazing. Papa was in his rocking chair on the hearth and everyone was settling in. The children formed a half-circle on the floor just in front of Papa – waiting expectantly.

Papa always began with a little history of what he called "a great line of storytellers." "It warms the people up," he always told Holly, "so that they settle down and prepare to listen."

Papa began, "I am, as many of you know, the Twentieth North Pole Santa, the twentieth in a long line of storytellers." With that, he launched into trip down memory lane, telling of being a child sitting on his own father's knee, where he learned about the long line of North Pole Santas and their storytelling abilities. "Storytellers," Papa said, "don't just read stories or repeat words. They bring stories to life using their voices, their facial expressions and through gestures." Then Papa made a big flourish in the air with his hands, making everyone laugh. "Even when he isn't telling the Christmas stories, he is a great storyteller," Holly thought.

"But," Papa continued, "what really makes my stories special is that they are always, always," he repeated, "true stories. "There's no reason to make stories up, when the true ones are so good," Papa laughed. "That's why they are so easy to tell!" He stopped and slowly looked around the room and into the eyes of each child that sat in front of him.

"Well, by golly, if you all don't look like to want to hear a story," Papa shouted, causing all the children to cheer. Papa slapped his legs and nearly jumped out of his rocker. "All right then. Let's start with one of Holly's favorite," and seeing Holly he gave her a wink, touched his finger to the side of his nose and began.

"Gather close, little ones. Because this story is for you, especially if you haven't heard it before." The children crowded onto the floor warmed by the fireplace and sat perfectly still, waiting to hear stories from the most famous of all storytellers, Holly's Papa.

Being a good storyteller, Papa knew that the children must not only listen, but they must participate in the story to make it exciting for them, so he said, "Those of you who have heard the stories before must help me tell the story from time to time. If I forget something, you must fill in the blank," he told them and a great "Yeay!" went up among those children already knowing the stories. That's how Papa involved all the children in his storytelling — and the parents were appreciative of his great gift.

"The story I'm going to tell first is about the elves – the official Christmas …" and Papa paused as if trying to remember a word and suddenly half the children yelled out "Toy makers!" and Papa responded, "Toy makers, yes, of course, how could I forget—toy makers!"

The children were roaring with excitement now — some because they already knew the story – the rest because they wanted to know the story. So Papa began the story in his very own way, occasionally "forgetting" a very important word, which would be filled in by children who had heard the stories before and were excited to be a part of telling it again.

"The very first North Pole Santa," Papa began, "came to the Arctic region, somewhere near North Pole, many, many years ago. In fact, it was 20 generations ago – and that's a very long time since, as you know, Santa's live very, very long lives.

The very first North Pole Santa decided to move to the North Pole because the Magic Reindeer lived nearby, and you all know that Magic Reindeer are very important to Santa. The Arctic is very cold, so not much lives there, but the Magic Reindeer must live in the region, because that's where they get their magic ability to…hmmm."

And the children knowing the story yelled out "fly!" and Papa responded, "Fly! Why, yes, of course." Then Papa asked the children, "Do you know any other reindeer that can fly?" They all shook their heads, indicating that they did not. Papa always asked that question – so that the children realized how special it was that the Magic Reindeer could fly, while other deer do not. Then he continued his story.

"North Pole Santa decided that the Magic Reindeer needed to be taken care of all year 'round, and since they could not live anywhere else it was only natural that he should go to live with them. So he and his young wife moved to the Arctic. Of course, they really hadn't realized just how cold it was, but they were young, willing and eager. Later, though, North Pole Santa and his wife moved a little further south, where it wasn't quite as cold but where the Magic Reindeer could live, too.

It wasn't long after North Pole Santa's arrival that he learned of some odd little characters that lived beneath the deep, deep ice of the North Pole." At this, some of the children started to look frightened, while the ones already knowing the story were nearly bouncing off the floor, because they knew they would get a chance to yell out what Papa would conveniently forget.

Papa went on with the story, watching their excitement building. "Because of their strange appearance – they had eyes that were perfectly round and way too large for their small faces, toes that curled to a point and ears that really looked like they belonged on an elephant — the people of the region made fun of them." Papa stopped here and looked at the children and added, "And that is not a nice thing to do, is it?" And the children all shook their heads and quietly said, "No, Santa," and Papa continued. "So these …"

"Elves" the children yelled, and Papa repeated, "Yes, elves, as they called themselves, created their own community below the ice".

"In fact, they lived below the ice for so long that they a built a complete community dozens of feet below the surface. They seldom were required to come out and didn't, except to gather food stores and to trade. While the people ridiculed these elves for their appearance, no one faulted their toy-making skills. The elves were wonderful toy-makers. They could fulfill any request with great skill."

"It was through a chance discovery of an almost lifelike toy soldier that the elves had made that North Pole Santa developed a friendship that would go beyond his own lifetime and into future generations of Santas."

"Living so far from civilization, North Pole Santa wasn't exactly sure how to get the toys he needed for the children of the Believing World at Christmas. At a time when he was getting quite concerned about the situation, he saw a brightly colored toy soldier towering above him in the snow. He was quite startled when he first saw it. The tall soldier looked as if he was ready to march across the frozen tundra."

"'Where on earth did you come from?'" North Pole Santa asked the solider. "'Could you really have marched here?' Suddenly North Pole Santa heard a giggle — and then another — coming from an ice cave that opened only a few feet from the soldier. Taking a few large steps he bent down and peeked into the cave, where to his utter amazement he discovered two tiny, tiny children with some very large eyes, elephant-like ears and a high pitched, contagious laugh." The listening children simply couldn't contain themselves now and blurted out. "It was the elves," and Papa just grinned and continued the story.

"Before he could say anything, they came bounding out of the ice cave, nearly knocking North Pole Santa to the ground. They were jumping and bubbling over with glee until North Pole Santa finally got them settled down enough to answer some questions – like who are you, where do you live and where did this toy soldier come from. After answering North Pole Santa's questions, the children went back into the cave, which was actually an entrance into their underground community. North Pole Santa was not allowed to go in, but the children assured him that they would bring their parents out, and that they did. In short order, North Pole Santa was surrounded by strange little characters whose parents were not much bigger than the children themselves and whose curiosity matched his own.

"Well, you know the rest," Papa said to the children, and they all shook their heads up and down in unison. "The elves have been the official toy-makers for Christmas ever since." Sounding quite final, Papa waited to see that he had everyone's attention before adding, "Now, if you want to know, as most children do, about the elves' underground town, called Elfton, why that is another story altogether." Then he laughed, knowing that they would, of course, want to hear that one, too.

So the stories continued. It was a wonderful time for everyone, especially the children, which included many of children of the town folk. The evening passed quickly and before anyone was ready, it was time to go. "Tomorrow is Christmas Eve day, children, a busy time for the elves and the Santa Claus family. Sweet dreams, children," and Papa nodded his head, touched a finger to the side of his nose and quietly left the room.

The children, worn out by the day's activities, were hustled away by their parents for a good night's rest. And the children did, indeed, have sweet dreams filled with memories that would live with them forever.

Chapter VIb   The Weather Worsens

Denise Graham Zahn

The Legend of the Twenty-First North Pole Santa

The morning of December 24th, Papa was abruptly awakened by a sharp knocking on the door. Though Papa was an early riser, he wasn't expecting anyone at this early hour. The sun wouldn't be up for several hours yet. Nevertheless, he put on his glasses, calmed his wife, Merry, who was as startled as he, and went downstairs to answer the door.

Without hesitation he opened the door and found one of his neighbors frantically waving his hands and pointing toward his home. It was too dark for Papa to see, of course, so he beckoned Charlie in. "Charlie, Charlie, slow down," Papa said, as he motioned for him to calm down. "Tell me what's going on."

"Papa, it's never been this bad. You know it's never been this bad." Papa responded, "What are you talking about Charlie? Slow down, for Heaven's sake." "The snow, Papa! Why – haven't you heard it?"

"Charlie, how would I hear snow falling?"

"Papa, it's never been like this. My roof has caved in from the very weight of it, and it has happened throughout the town. Many of the town folk have no place to stay, Papa. I came to you for help. What are we going to do – and Christmas Eve is tonight. Oh, how terrible. I don't know what to do!"

"Well, the first thing you need to do is calm down. Let's get you some hot apple cider, and I'll call my wife down. She'll want to help."

Of course, Merry was already up and in the kitchen fixing the hot cider. She had heard the conversation and knew she would be needed. Fortunately, their own home was as solid as a rock, but they would need to arrange space for some of their neighbors. Unfortunately, the Santas and their families that had already arrived were occupying most of the rooms in their home. Nonetheless, they would not turn anyone away who needed help. Merry would see to it.

As the hours approached daylight, Papa's house began to reach full capacity. But at least when daylight arrived, the damages throughout the town could be assessed so a plan could be made. The question was, how long would the snow continue and how many more families would have to leave their homes. It remained to be seen. In the meanwhile, Papa and Mama made everyone feel at home. The pantry was stocked, so all the friends and neighbors with their children

The Legend of the Twenty-First North Pole Santa

enjoyed a warm breakfast and were calmed by the knowledge that they were there for each other. The children, of course, had fallen asleep on comforters in the great room beneath the portrait of the First North Pole Santa.

At first light Papa began to awaken those who had at last fallen asleep. "Listen, men, my wife has prepared breakfast for you. Once you've eaten, go home and check the damage done to your homes. Let your wives and children sleep. In the meantime, I will find out about weather predictions. Come back once you've done what you can to protect your homes. We'll have a hearty meal ready for you."

Papa was concerned about the homes of the town folk but no one was hurt and he knew that they would help each other out. "There really isn't a lot they can do until the weather clears," he said to Mama and Holly, who were busy fixing breakfast. Looking out the window he shook his head slowly and said quietly, "It just keeps coming down."

Then he turned to Merry and said, "Mama, take a look. It is so thick that you can't see more than a few feet in front of you, and the wind is fierce." Then, dropping the curtain over the window, Papa prepared to go outside. "I must get to the airport," he said to Mama abruptly, who knew what he was thinking. Holly knew also and insisted that she go along and Mama agreed.

Papa's real concern, of course, was Christmas. Many of the Santas had not yet arrived. Without all the Santas, they would not be able to deliver the gifts, even with Rudy guiding the way. The Believing World was simply too large after twenty generations of Santas, who lived very long lives. How would they make the Christmas deliveries?

After feeding the Magic Reindeer, Papa and Holly prepared Rudy for the ride. Flying didn't seem necessary for the short distance to the airport, after all. "Holly," Papa said, when they were on the road, "These roads are impassable for anything but the Magic Reindeer. I have never seen it this bad. I don't hold much hope that the Santas will make it to the Fairbanks Airport."

Papa was right. All flights had been cancelled, both incoming and outgoing. Accustomed to cold, the airport simply could not keep up with this snow especially with the wind swirling it into deep drifts. Papa was very concerned now, but he knew that his neighbors required immediate help, so he turned his focus to that. But it was difficult to forget that Christmas Eve was just hours away.

"Little Star," Papa said, "if the snow does not stop soon, the Santas won't arrive in time to deliver presents to the children tonight — something I don't want to think about — not now, anyway." Then he abruptly changed the subject. "We've got to get back to help Mama."

The possibility that there really might not be a Christmas for the first time ever was more than he could bear to think of. How could they break the hearts of children all over the world? Papa's strength amazed Holly, his heart had already been broken by the news that Holly would not to receive her birthright, and now Christmas might be cancelled altogether.

"No," Holly thought. "That won't happen. Papa will not let Christmas be cancelled. He will find a way, even if he himself doesn't think so." Holly had confidence in Papa and put her arm through his and said nothing.

After the town folk had lunch, everyone headed to the town hall where a meeting was called. More people than he expected were there when he arrived. "Santa," one of them spoke up, "There is so much damage to nearly every home throughout the town that there is little we can do to help each other. Few homes were spared and with visitors in town for the holidays, all the hotels and motels are full. We don't know where to wait it out. The town hall isn't meant for these kinds of situations."

Papa listened and shook his head. They were right, and he had no idea what to do. And his thoughts kept turning to the possibility of canceling Christmas. Suddenly, though, like a spark, Papa's face lit up, surprising everyone. Pointing a finger, he turned quickly to Holly and said, "Little Star, go to Elfton and wake up Ely. Tell him I need him here as quickly as possible – don't delay."

Off Holly flew and whisked Ely back to the town hall – barely letting him dress. Breathless, Ely arrived with Little Star to see the town hall full of people without hope — with one exception.

"Ely, thank you for coming so quickly. We need your help," Papa said. The town folk looked confused, but Papa continued. "The roofs on these people's homes have caved in from the snow, and they have no where to stay. Every place, including my home, is full." He looked straight at Ely, knowing that what he was going to ask was a big favor

– a favor that only Papa could have asked and expected to get agreement on.

Ely knew something big was coming, but he could not have predicted what Papa was going to ask him. Papa blurted out, "Ely…can they stay in Elfton?"

Well, this was a first. No one but elves had ever stayed in Elfton, and Ely thought that this was not a good precedent. After all, he thought, my ancestors were treated very poorly, very poorly, by the town folk. Besides, maybe they should have built their homes underground, where it's safe! Absolutely. They should have built underground homes.

Papa could read Ely's face before he even opened his mouth, so it was no surprise when he responded, "Santa, it's never been done, never ever been done, and we are very busy right now, very busy, with last minute toy making," he said, as if that would be the final word – which it was not.

"Ely," replied Papa, "These people need our help – and isn't that what the spirit of Christmas is about—giving to others from our hearts?" Ely was flustered now.

"Papa is definitely good," Holly thought. "He pushed the just the right button, and Ely responded in just the way Papa knew that he would." Holly smiled.

By now Ely was struggling, not with the decision but to keep his excitement in. Suddenly he burst out yelling, "Why, yes. Yes!" he said. "Of course! It most certainly is Christmas. Most certainly," he said, rubbing his chin. Suddenly his hands flew up and he yelled over the crowded room "Of course, of course, you may stay with us." And with that, a huge grin covered his tiny face, and the spirit of the town folk was restored.

Papa heaved a huge sigh of relief, even though he always knew that Ely would most certainly – most certainly help.

Papa hugged Ely, flustering him a little, but he was calmed when Papa said, "Thank you Ely, you are a true friend to the community. Now I must figure out what we can do about Christmas."

Papa left the town hall and headed for home, which remained full of town folk and family. "Canceling Christmas is out of the question," he told Mama and Holly. "Most certainly out of the question," he said with a grin, thinking back to Ely. Mama was confused, but Holly

The Legend of the Twenty-First North Pole Santa

smiled knowingly. Papa winked at her. "What can we do to deliver the gifts with so few Santas to run the sleighs?" Papa asked them both. Mama and Holly just looked at each other. They had no ideas for Papa this time. "Well," Papa said, "I guess it's time for a Powwow with my family."

Denise Graham Zahn

Chapter VII Santa Family Powwow

Denise Graham Zahn

Papa stepped into the great hall to find three of his brothers with their sons waiting for him. They, too, knew the dilemma, and had been discussing what to do.

"Herald," Uncle Noel said as Papa came through the door, "I'm glad you are here, and I'm very appreciative that the elves agreed to help the town folk. It is a generous gesture and a tribute to their friendship with you." Papa, now a little flustered himself, knowing he had walked into a room where clearly some decisions were being made replied with an embarrassed, "Yes, I am very pleased with the elves and happy for the town folk. It is a relief." He paused, waiting for his brother to continue with an explanation of what had been going on.

"Herald, the situation is critical. We simply do not have enough Santas here to deliver all the gifts to the Believing World. There is no way around it." Papa agreed. "The question is" Uncle Noel continued, "What do we do about it?" Papa responded with, "Actually, I was just coming to discuss the same matter. Do you have any ideas?" Papa's attitude relieved everyone. It truly was a family matter, and this was Papa's family.

Uncle Noel then felt comfortable in continuing, "Yes, Herald, we believe we do. In fact, we believe it's the only solution to the dilemma. Let me tell you about it."

Papa was relieved that there was a solution being proposed, because he just had no more time to think about it himself. He really had wanted to talk to his brother Noel about the situation with Holly but there had been no time for that, either. But he was sure that the right time would present itself. In the meantime, though, he wanted to hear their idea. "Yes, please do tell me. I'll be happy for a solution."

Just then Holly walked in. She saw that a conference was going on, so she came in quietly, but not without being noticed by Uncle Noel, Papa and Nicky. Uncle Noel continued on, however, without comment on her arrival. "Herald, if all the delayed Santas can get to Anchorage then we can go get them with you and Rudy leading the way. We can fly enough sleighs to pick them up and bring them back."

Papa thought a minute. "That's a wonderful idea, but we don't have enough Santas here to run the sleighs to pick them up." Noel hesitated. He knew this would be sensitive. He glanced quickly

The Legend of the Twenty-First North Pole Santa

around the room to see if Holly was still present. She was – and listening intently. "Herald, what we would need to do is move up the initiation time for the new Santas."

"Ah," Papa sighed, clearly understanding that the initiation would not include his daughter. Holly also understood, and Papa turned to her. Holly nodded to her father, giving quiet approval to her father, understanding his dilemma. Uncle Noel saw the sadness in both of their faces as Papa replied, "Then that is what we will have to do."

Holly stood up and said, "I will start making the arrangements to get all the Santas to the Anchorage Airport." "Thank you, Holly," Uncle Noel said, "You have a wonderful spirit." Holly responded without anger, "Thank you, Uncle Noel. I take after Mama and Papa." Uncle Noel winced ever so slightly.

Chapter IX Show Time

Denise Graham Zahn

Usually the initiation took place after the gifts were loaded and the Santas were ready to take off to deliver them. This year would be different. Like so many years before when Rudy had guided the reindeer through the fog, this night he would be needed to guide many sleighs and reindeer to the Anchorage Airport to pick up the remaining Santas and soon-to-be Santas. They would leave their families in Anchorage until the blizzard stopped, and then hop a plane to the Fairbanks Airport.

Papa had not forgotten that he meant to have a conversation with Noel before the Christmas Eve deliveries, but the right time still had not arrived. The blizzard continued its fury. The snowflakes were so large you could see the individual patterns, and the wind whipped furiously around and between the buildings like small tornadoes, stinging the eyes and any exposed skin. It was as beautiful as it was dangerous.

Papa was in the barn getting Rudy ready for the early flight. "Rudy, old fellow," he told him, "This is a new one for both of us. I know you can do it, though we've never been in a storm this bad. But if you lead, the others will follow," and Papa was quite sure that what he said was true.

Papa continued his conversation with Rudy. "While I have confidence in you, Rudy, it is not a good night for newly initiated Santas to be running the sleighs on their own. Usually they have the benefit of having one of the experienced Santas to ride with them. Tonight, we will rely more on the experience of the reindeer and hope they can see you." Thinking that he sounded more negative than he intended, Papa added, "The new Santas are well-trained, though, and this is what they were trained for."

"OK. Time is running out," Papa thought. "If we don't leave soon, despite the weather, we won't make it back to the North Pole in time to load up the remaining presents and get them delivered tonight." Holly had come in, and Papa asked her to get the others. "Tell them it is time," Papa said. "We can't wait any longer for a break in the weather."

After delivering the message, Holly returned to the barn to wait with Papa and Rudy. Holly had brushed Rudy's heavy coat till it glistened, in preparation for this special night – a night that should have been hers to remember forever. It should have been the night when she was initiated and given her birthright of being designated as Twenty-First North Pole Santa. Papa was thinking about that when Holly touched his arm. She knew what was going on.

"Papa, don't worry about it. It will work out. I know it will," she said.

"You are right, Little Star. Things do have a way of working out – even when you can't see it yet. You are my Little Star, Holly, and Mama and I are thankful everyday that you came into our lives." Papa hugged her tightly and Rudy bellowed approval. They were still laughing when Papa's brothers and nephews arrived.

"Let's get this show on the road," Papa gleamed. "Let's go, Rudy," Holly said as she led him out of the barn to the waiting sleigh. The other reindeer were already harnessed and hooked-up to their sleighs and waiting outside the barn.

"Santas, you know the process. Climb aboard a sleigh and invite an initiate with you." Papa, climbed aboard Rudy's sleigh, but instead of asking Holly to climb up with him, as it should have been, he asked one of his nephews. "OK, Joseph. It's time." Joseph's smile couldn't have been bigger, despite the awful weather conditions. Truth be told, the youngsters, inexperienced as they were, were quite ignorant of the danger the weather presented and thought it was going to be a great adventure.

"I'm ready, Uncle Herald," he said as he stepped up onto the bench in the sleigh and sat beside his uncle. "Now, Santas," Papa said, shouting over the wind to be heard, "take the reins in your hands." Knowing the ritual already, the Santas picked up the reins from the elves standing beside the reindeer. Papa stood up in preparation of making the formal pronouncement to hand over of the reins to the initiates, proclaiming them official Santas of the Believing World.

"Santas, you are gift bearers to the Believing World. You deliver gifts and happiness, but this responsibility is truly a gift given to you for a lifetime. As you have been taught – all that you give and more — will be returned to you in joy! Live joyously!" Papa paused a moment to look at each expectant face, with smiles that glowed through glistening, blowing snow.

"Initiates – take …." And before Papa could finish the sentence, the barn door, ripped from its hinges by the wind, struck Papa full

The Legend of the Twenty-First North Pole Santa

force, and swept him up like a magic carpet. Before anyone even realized what had happened, the barn door then flipped over, dumping Papa off as quickly as it had picked him up.

It happened so fast that no one had time to react until Holly heard her father's voice coming from the side of the barn where huge snowdrifts had built up. "Holly! Holly!" he was calling, but she couldn't see him. It seemed forever, but within a minute her uncles and cousins were searching the area where his voice echoed. "Papa, keep calling us. We hear you but can't find you," she yelled over the screaming wind. He called again and Holly pinpointed where his voice was coming from.

"He's over here, everyone. Help me!" she called to the others. "Let's get him out," she screamed, beginning to panic.

"Wait." Holly heard a voice coming from behind her. It was her cousin Jose, from Mexico. He continued, "Wait, Holly. Let's use snow-shovels and dig a wide path to him. But don't touch him when you reach him. He might be injured, and we don't want to make it worse." During the off-season (so to speak) Jose was a nurse, and Holly trusted him.

"OK, Jose, but please, let's hurry," Holly replied.

"Papa, we're here, Papa," she cried to her father. "Holly. Holly," he responded with little energy. Nicky and her other cousins and uncles were shoveling. The wind blowing around the corner of the barn had created a sand dune of snow. Close to the barn the ground was bare, but about 15 feet further out the snow swept up as high as the base of the roof. Her father had landed in the deepest part.

It was difficult shoveling because the snow was so deep and still coming down, but her cousins worked as fast as they could with snow-shovels from the barn. From the barn they dug a path to where her father was. Holly hoped that the depth of the snow had broken his fall so that he wasn't hurt, but she was afraid it hadn't.

Jose went in when a pathway was cleared. "Uncle Herald," he said. "Are you hurt?"

"Holly. Jose. What happened? Is Christmas over? Have I been dreaming? Why do my legs hurt? Where am I?" Papa asked.

"Oh, Papa." Holly cried. "It was awful, Papa, but you'll be OK," and as she said those words she turned to Jose to see if what she had just told her Papa was true. Jose did not look at her. He just continued to examine his uncle.

"I feel like I was hit by a barn door, Holly," Papa whispered weakly. "Well, Papa," she replied, "you were," and everyone laughed despite themselves.

Jose interrupted. "Holly, you must get your mother and call for an ambulance. Your father's leg is broken near the ankle. He seems OK otherwise, but we must get him to the hospital to check for other injuries, those I can't see." Holly suddenly looked stricken. Already the shoveled path was filling in. She immediately jumped up and ran as fast as she could through the snow to find her mother. "How will an ambulance get here through this blizzard," she wondered, as she ran.

Jose was trying to awaken Papa, who had passed out, when Holly and her mother arrived. Mama was calm – at least outwardly – and knelt beside her husband. "Papa. Papa. Wake up. You have presents to deliver tonight," she said, knowing full well that he could not – not this year – but also knowing that if anything could bring him around that would be it. She was right.

Mama's voice was exactly what Papa needed. He was now conscious but slightly dazed. "Help me get up, Jose. We must leave soon or we will run out of time."

Jose responded, "Uncle Herald. You cannot go. Not tonight. Tonight we must get you to a doctor." But at that point Mama spoke up. "Jose," she said, "We are going to have to rely on your experience until the weather breaks. The hospital said the ambulance couldn't possibly get here through the deep snow and…" her voice cracked and trailed off into the whistling wind. It was not a good situation.

While Jose was confident he could splint Papa's leg, the break appeared simple, he was concerned about Papa passing out and that he might have critical internal injuries.

Papa interrupted Jose's thoughts, taking control, even when he was down. "OK, Jose," Papa piped up, "I am in your hands. What do we need to do?"

"Uncle Herald, I have a suggestion. I can splint your leg, but you need a doctor and some tests to determine if you have any other injuries. You passed out on me, you know," and Jose forced a little smile. Then, a real smile appeared on Jose's face.

"Here's what we can do, Uncle Herald," the words tumbled out. "The reindeer are ready to go. If we can complete the initiation, we will just turn Rudy's sleigh into a temporary ambulance and drop you off at the hospital as we head to Anchorage."

Holly was elated. "What a wonderful idea, Cousin Jose," she shouted over the wind. "Let's do it, Papa. What do you think, Mama?"

"I think I'm going, too. That's what I think." Mama replied, giving Holly a hug and again kneeling down beside her husband. "Are you ready, Papa?"

"Yes, Mama. Let's finish the initiation, and you and Holly can go to the hospital with me."

"Jose. Do what you have to, so I can finish the initiation and we can get going."

With that, Jose and the others searched the barn to find a makeshift gurney on which to carry his uncle. He also found a board for splinting his leg, while Mama brought strips of sheets for wrapping. She offered Papa aspirin for the pain. He managed a little smile.

"Thank you, Mama, I don't think it will quite do the job, but thank you. Holding your hand will be the best medicine I could ask for."

"We're ready, Uncle Herald," Jose said. After splinting his leg they lifted Papa onto the gurney and carried him to the back of the sleigh where they opened the back and slid him in, followed by Mama and Holly on either side.

"You're on, Uncle Herald!" Jose yelled as he secured the back of the sleigh.

Chapter X On to Anchorage

Denise Graham Zahn

The Legend of the Twenty-First North Pole Santa

"Back to your sleighs everyone. We've delayed long enough," Papa shouted. Once everyone was again in place, Papa again instructed the Santas to take the reins and repeated what he said earlier. The next step was the official moment – the moment each initiate had waited for. Papa yelled as best he could, "This is the moment when your destinies will be fulfilled, young men, for as long as you live."

"All right, Santas. Pass the reins to the next generation," he shouted again, his heart overwhelmed with emotion, as it was each year, except this year it was mixed with a deep sadness.

At once, as each initiate took the reins, a transformation took place. These young men, each having reached a full 16 years of age, began to change. Knowing this was coming, they pulled out their pocket mirrors and watched as their hair turned snowy white, and where only peach fuzz had been, a full wavy, white beard grew. This was the transformation that each had anxiously awaited. They were joyous and exuberant. They whooped and hollered and hugged.

Sitting beside her father and across from her mother, Holly also waved, but her parents knew – along with Nicky – that her heart was breaking. One other person was watching Holly, too. It was her Uncle Noel. Though they could not see it, a silent tear streaked down his face.

"It's time to roll," Papa shouted. "You've got work to do now. Nicky, won't you guide my sleigh tonight?" Papa quipped in an attempt to remain cheerful.

"Of course," Uncle Herald. "I'd be proud to guide Rudy and," he whispered closely so only they cold hear, "my favorite aunt, uncle and cousin."

"Let's go then," Papa said, as he reached his hand up to touch Nicky's hand for just a moment. Nicky was ready, and the others were in place, as well. The reindeer had long been ready, except for Rudy, who had been snorting and stomping. Holly knew that he was upset by the incident and had never had anyone but North Pole Santa's family handling his reins. She had tried to calm him before climbing in the sleigh with her mother and father, but he was still restless and resisting.

Holly nodded to Nicky to go ahead. "Reindeer ready? Santas ready?" he yelled. Each of the Santas, including the new Santas on their sleighs nodded that their reindeer were ready. Nicky looked at Rudy and said, "OK, Rudy, calm down. We're taking Papa to the hospital, you know."

Again Nicky shouted, "Santas ready?" Instantly each of the Santas broke into a grin as big as the snowstorm and raised their right thumbs in a signal that they were ready and anxious. "To Anchorage," he shouted to Rudy – but nothing happened. "Come on Rudy," he shouted again, "Let's head to the hospital." Rudy didn't budge. After several more attempts at getting Rudy to move, Nicky turned to Papa.

"What are we going to do, Uncle Herald? Rudy has no intention of allowing me to lead." Holly jumped out of the sleigh and ran to Rudy. "Rudy. What's wrong, boy? We have to get Papa to the hospital and head to Anchorage." Hearing Holly's voice again, Rudy snuggled his muzzle under her arm in affection. It was clear to everyone that there was a very special bond between Rudy and Holly.

While Holly comforted Rudy, Nicky purposefully walked over to his father, who had been watching with concern.

"Father," Nicky said, "This is not right. Rudy will obviously only go if Holly has the reins and Holly cannot hold the reins unless she is initiated."

"Son, I believe you may be right, but that is not my only concern. Let's talk to your uncle. Together Uncle Noel and Nicky approached Papa. Holly saw them coming and knew something was up. She said nothing, just listened.

"Herald," Uncle Noel said, "I know you wanted to talk and the time never came. I also know that you believe I want my son to be North Pole Santa out of selfishness. While I will be very proud for my son to receive the honor, that is not my primary motivation. I know that you believe Holly is truly your daughter — spiritually, if not by birth. I admire you for your commitment. But have you thought about how devastated Holly will be when the transformation doesn't happen? Wouldn't it be better not to put her in that position?

"Herald," he said, and paused, "despite your hopes and dreams for Holly. She is not a natural born Santa. The transformation won't take place, and she will be devastated.

Papa was so relieved. He had truly believed his brother's motives were selfish. It was wonderful to know that it wasn't the case – and Papa could deal with this.

"Noel, you are my brother, and I love you and trust you – but in this you are wrong. Holly was doubly blessed, first as the daughter of her Athabascan parents and then to come to Mama and I. She is a very special gift. She is as much a part of the Santa family as her cousins."

Then Nicky spoke up, "Father, shouldn't Holly have the right to take that risk if she chooses to?" Uncle Noel turned to face Holly, who had been listening quietly. "Well, Holly, are you are willing to take the risk? I certainly don't have an alternative to offer at this point. We need to get your father to the hospital and get these reindeer moving. How do you feel about it?"

Holly could hardly contain herself. She was overjoyed. She jumped out of the sleigh and ran to her uncle, but he cut her short with a word of caution. "Holly, I am very serious about my concerns. Please, consider what I have said. I love you, child, but because the natural genetic lineage isn't there, I think you are in for a huge disappointment. Can you handle it?"

"But Uncle Noel," Holly quipped, "I am a Santa. My birth parents would want this for me. I will make them proud, and I will make Mama and Papa proud. I will make you proud, too. Just wait and see. I will make the transformation, just like my cousins."

"Holly, just one more word of caution. Please don't be heartbroken if it doesn't. We all love you, anyway," and he hugged Holly tightly before stepping away. Then, taking a deep breath he proclaimed, "All right. Let's do it. Papa, are you up to handling another initiation?"

"I wouldn't miss it, Noel – and thank you," he added warmly. With Mama's help, Papa sat up a little in the sleigh, while Uncle Noel took the reins beside Holly. Going through the same ritual as he had earlier, the time came for Uncle Noel to hand the reins off to Holly.

Holly was exuberant. Papa and Mama were as proud and happy as they had ever been. Uncle Noel was nervous as was Nicky, and the others simply waited to see what would happen in the next few moments. They didn't know who was right. This was a first, after all. But they all wished the best for Holly and knew in their hearts she was as much a cousin to them as they were to each other – but because of that they didn't want her hurt.

The Legend of the Twenty-First North Pole Santa

The moment was tense as Papa said "All right, Santa, pass the reins to the next generation." Uncle Noel only paused a second before handing the reins to Holly. With no hesitation Holly took the reins from her uncle and before the blink of an eye or the next beat of her heart her long black Athabascan hair turned snowy white and wavy. She didn't need a mirror to tell her she had made the change. She knew it by watching the expectant faces of Papa, Mama, Uncle Noel, her other uncles and her cousins. But it was Nicky who spoke first.

"Little Star, you are shining brighter than any star in the universe tonight. You are truly a Santa." Without pause he continued, "Now let's get rolling. We've a busy night ahead of us."

"Just one second, Holly Santa Claus," piped in Uncle Noel, "I am relieved child, and very happy that I had no reason to fear for you. You make a fine Santa, but I must say I'm quite glad that you didn't grow a beard."

Uncle Noel then turned to Papa and Mama, "She's our Little Star, all right!"

Chapter XI Rudy

Denise Graham Zahn

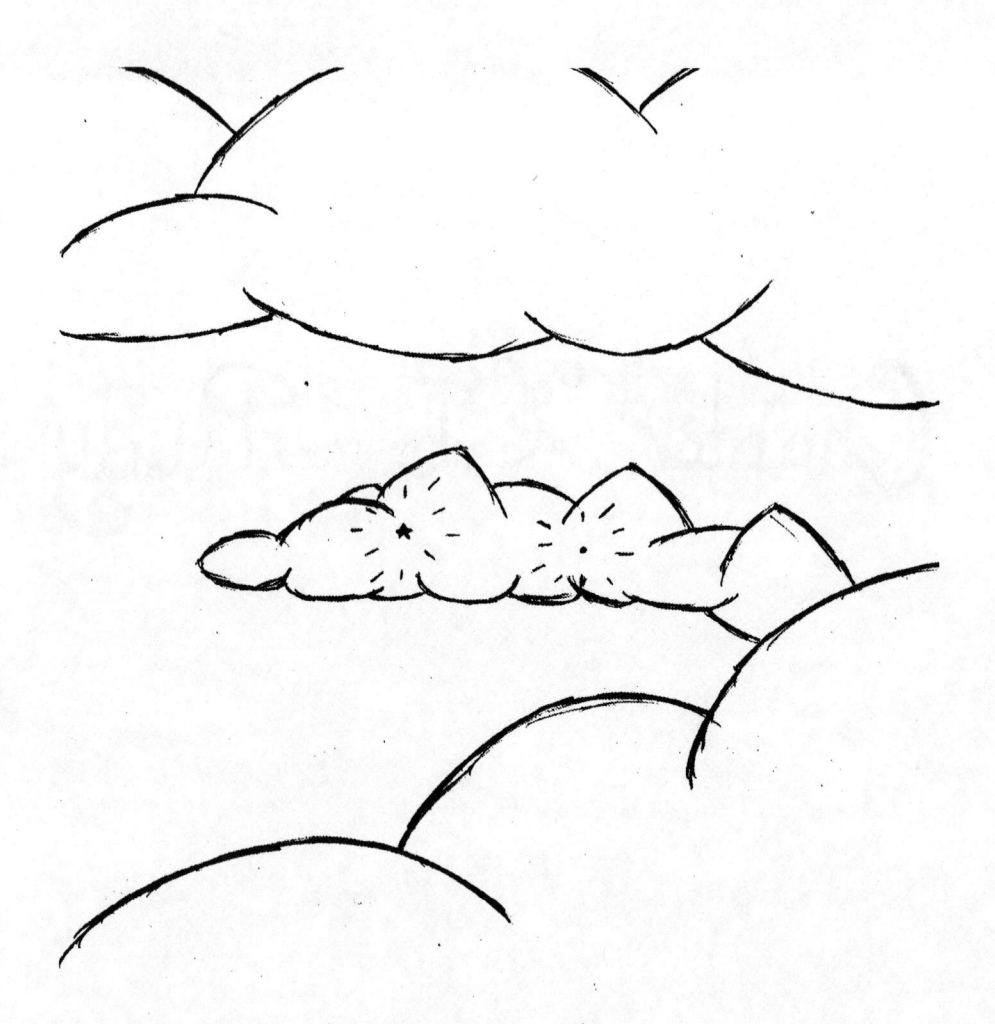

The Legend of the Twenty-First North Pole Santa

Once again everyone was in place. This time Holly held Rudy's reins, and she was taking her Mama and Papa to the hospital – and then on to Anchorage to pick up the snowed out Santas. After snuggling his nose in Holly's arms, Rudy settled down and was ready to lead his fellow Magic Reindeer. "Oh, Rudy," Holly whispered, "Thank you for being so stubborn."

Now it was Holly's turn to get things moving. With the snow still heavy and the wind still howling, she shouted, "Let's roll, reindeer. Onward, all you Santas," and off they flew. One by one the reindeer took off with their sleighs – some in the hands of experienced Santas—others under the charge of the newly appointed Santas. It was a very special moment, unlike any that had ever been, and Holly and Rudy were in the lead.

They took off north, headed into the wind, and then curved back to head southeast. They had just taken off, it seemed, when they caught sight of the hospital. The entire roof had been cleared of the still falling snow and a large spotlight shined into the dark sky, helping them find the way. With ease Rudy and Holly landed the sleigh. This was a team. There was no necessity to discover each other's patterns.

It was as if they had flown together forever, and it didn't go unnoticed by Uncle Noel and his brothers. It was another sign that this was the way it was meant to be.

While Papa and Mama were transported into the hospital, the remaining Santas and reindeer flew in circles overhead. Some observant children noticed it and were sent scurrying to bed by their parents, who saw an opportunity to get them to bed early. "Oh, my, they said to the children. You had better get to sleep quickly, or Santa won't stop at our house." Of course, the children didn't look at the clock. They just headed straight to bed without fussing a bit.

Saying her good-byes to Papa and Mama, Holly took off with Rudy as smoothly as they had landed. Again the train of sleighs headed southeast, — next stop— the Anchorage Airport to pick up all the Santas and initiates who were held back by the storm.

Reports had been that the storm was heading east from North Pole, and perhaps it was, but if that were the case, then another storm had struck as well, for the further south they went the heavier the snow became. Rudy's leadership (and, of course, his nose) and his bond with Holly is all that enabled them to stay on course. Holly, too, instinctively knew which was the right way to go. Some of the new Santas were having more difficulty.

Because they lived away from the North Pole, they had not developed their intuition or a bond with the reindeer, so they were struggling to communicate. It was important for them to stay close to Rudy and Holly and to each other. In this blizzard, they could easily get lost for hours, and time was important. It was already Christmas Eve, and they still had to return to the North Pole to pick up the presents.

No sooner had Holly thought about the others staying close than she looked back and could see the faint outline of only several sleighs. "Oh, Rudy," she cried. "We've lost them. We must turn back." But up ahead she could also see the runway lights of the airport. Feeling Rudy's unwillingness to turn back, Holly said, "You're right, Rudy. Let's get these guys on the ground, then you and I will go back to find the others."

The airport was prepared for them. The storm was hitting here, too, but the runway had been cleared. The Santas and initiates were ready and waiting to be picked up, but it was quickly noticed that only a few sleighs had landed.

Before they had time to ask questions, Holly told them that she and Rudy were heading back to find the others. In this case, they would have to rely on Rudy's nose and experience to help them find the others. Uncle Noel and Nicky said they would take care of everything on the ground and would let Papa and Mama know what was going on. "Be careful Holly," Uncle Noel said, "and find them soon," he said to Rudy, knowing that time was quickly running out. If they didn't get back to North Pole soon, Christmas would be missed.

Only the glow of Rudy's nose could be seen in the distance. Uncle Noel hoped that would be enough to guide the others to them. In the meantime, all they could do was wait and be prepared to leave quickly should they get back in time.

Holly and Rudy had been searching the sky for the wayward reindeer and their drivers with no success. "This is like looking for a needle in a haystack, Rudy," she sighed. "But we must find them. We have no choice. We simply cannot miss Christmas."

Then she stopped abruptly, deciding she needed to clear her mind. "Just give me a minute while I close my eyes, Rudy" she said. But Holly wasn't going to sleep. She was reaching inside herself to find her connection with the others. In the shake of a lamb's tail she declared confidently, "We're going to find them, Rudy, and instantly she knew which way to go. Without a word, Rudy headed that way. "Oh, Rudy," she yelled. "You read my mind!"

The others had veered off course, headed west. "Let's go, Rudy, and fast," Holly commanded. Smooth as ice, Rudy made the turn, his nose a beacon of light, but Holly's heart directing the way. "What a team we are!" she thought.

But they didn't find them. Something was wrong, Holly thought. "I know I felt them this way, Rudy. Where could they be?" Suddenly, they heard a "whoosh" as they were nearly run over by the leading sleigh followed by all the others.

When Holly and Rudy realized this was the missing sleigh train, they turned and pulled ahead of them. Her cousin in the lead sleigh yelled, "Sorry, about that Holly. We misjudged the distance. We're so glad you found us. We were still heading the wrong direction when we saw Rudy gleaming in the dark. And not only that, we saw something that glowed very much like a little star behind him – and it was you, Holly! You really glow like a little star."

Holly was pleased, and she could feel that Rudy was more relaxed. "Let's fly, you guys," Holly shouted, "and keep your eye on the little red bouncing ball," referring to Rudy's nose. "You got it, Little Star," her cousin replied.

In no time, they were back at the airport, much to the relief of Uncle Noel and the others. The "Snowed-Out Santas", as Holly had decided to call them because she thought it added a little humor to the situation, waved good-bye to their families and off they flew, heading to North Pole. Once the weather improved, the families would join the "Snowed-Out Santas" in North Pole, completing the rest of their trip by plane.

Chapter XII We're Back

Denise Graham Zahn

The Legend of the Twenty-First North Pole Santa

The elves were beginning to panic. Santa wasn't there and neither were Mama or Holly. They had no one to turn to, to find out what was going on, and if they didn't get back soon, they would miss Christmas and Believing Children of all sizes around the world would be disappointed, and the toys would have no homes to go to.

Ely was trying to keep them calm. "Most certainly," he muttered to himself and to the other elves, "most certainly Christmas has never been missed. What shall we do, if they don't arrive? What shall we do?" The question seemed to blow around in the wind and come back to Ely. He heard his own voice asking the question over and over, though he hadn't asked it but once – well, maybe twice. But this time, as the question came back to him he heard an answer.

"We're coming Ely. We're coming," it repeated. The voice was Holly's, and it was crystal clear, though not one elf could see them coming. There was no red glow in the sky to be seen – at least not yet.

But Ely was calm now, because he knew, despite the fact that he couldn't see them – that they were, indeed, coming. "Have a cup of wassail, everyone. They will be here soon. Be sure to share a cup with them, too, for they'll be cold for sure. Most certainly they'll be cold, and we must get them off quickly. Christmas is upon us. Yes, yes," he gleamed, "Christmas is most certainly upon us."

Well, all the elves knew that Ely was right. Though they couldn't see anything, Ely was always to be trusted. So they sat in the sleighs that they had loaded with toys and gifts and toasted each other and their many blessings with the wonderful, warm wassail. "This is," Ely said, "a Christmas different from all others. So much that went wrong, went right. Yes," he repeated, "What went wrong, went right. Remember that. Yes, Yes. Remember that," he said once more and fell asleep where he sat.

Moments later, or so it seemed, Ely was awakened by the shouts of the elves. "They're coming, Ely. We see Rudy's glowing nose and something shining like a little star just behind him. We don't know what it is, but it certainly looks like a little star."

Ely quickly arose and went to see for himself. "You are right. Be prepared to help them quickly. They must leave immediately or Christmas will be missed," and as he spoke he, too, saw the glow coming from behind Rudy and wondered what it might be.

With wassail steaming in the cups the elves waited anxiously for the arrival and soon the sleighs were within view, as miraculously the snow lessened so that just a few flakes remained floating in the air. "I see them, I see them," shouted one of the elves, and the clock in town began a chime that echoed as each strike told them how close it was to Christmas and how close they were coming to missing it entirely.

One by one the sleighs began to land, and the elves, searching for the glowing little star they had seen just behind Rudy, laughed aloud when they realized that it wasn't just a little star that they had seen – it was "Little Star." And no one was surprised. It was just another reason that they would remember this Christmas.

"Quickly. Quickly now, everyone. Santas, please rest a moment and drink your wassail, while we load your sleighs. We can't miss Christmas. We most certainly cannot," Ely babbled as he scurried about pointing here and there as the elves loaded the sleighs.

But there was one more step to be taken before the sleighs could take off. The initiates needed to be initiated, but Papa wasn't there to perform the ritual. "Father, Holly," said Nick. "Who is going to perform the initiation?"

Holly and Uncle Noel looked at each other. While Holly had been initiated, the question of whether or not she would receive her birthright as the Twenty-First North Pole Santa remained. Nicky, after all, had been told that he would receive the birthright, and the next North Pole Santa should perform the ritual.

"Father," Nicky started to say, but Holly interrupted. "Uncle Noel, why don't you take the honors. You are Papa's next younger brother, and Papa would be proud to have you take his place."

"Great idea," Nicky chimed in. Uncle Noel was slightly embarrassed, but the issue, at least, was put off a little longer. "I'd be honored," he said softly, then turned and shouted, "Santas and initiates climb aboard!" And the ritual was repeated for the third time that night.

"Noel, Holly, Nicky, you must go immediately or Christmas will most certainly be missed," urged Ely. "Go now. Right now, for Christmas most certainly cannot be missed," he added.

"OK, Ely," Holly responded. "We are most certainly going immediately. Right Uncle Noel and Nicky?"

The Legend of the Twenty-First North Pole Santa

"Most certainly," they chimed in together. Then Holly shouted, "Santas. Reindeer. It's Christmas! Let's make it a merry one for all the world, for even if not everyone believes in us, we believe in them!"

With that, off they flew into the clearing sky. If any child had peeked out the window that night, they would have seen a spectacular sight – a sky full of sleighs and Santas lead by Magical Reindeer, each heading to a different part of the world to deliver Christmas joy.

Chapter XIII Return Trip

Denise Graham Zahn

The Legend of the Twenty-First North Pole Santa

It was nearly dawn on Christmas morning when the last of the Santas and reindeer arrived back at North Pole. But Christmas would not be complete without Papa and Mama. Papa had been very lucky. The hospital complimented Jose on what he had done and put a cast on Papa's leg. There were no internal injuries. By late afternoon he was allowed to come home in a wheel chair, a minor inconvenience for one so lucky.

Rudy, Holly and Nicky flew to pick up Mama and Papa, who had already heard that Christmas had been a great success. Papa was very proud when he heard how Rudy and Holly had found the Santas and reindeer lost in the snowy, night sky.

"Do you know, Uncle Herald, that your Little Star has a glow of her own?" asked Nicky? "Why, what are you talking about, Nicky," Papa replied. "As Rudy and Holly approached the airport, we saw not only saw Rudy's shining nose but a glowing little star appeared behind him. It wasn't until their arrival that everyone saw that it was Little Star herself shining through the dark. The elves saw it, too. "She has a gift, uncle. She is a gift," he concluded.

"Why thank you for sharing that," Papa said, "but Mama and I have always seen her glow. I thought everyone did."

Back at the North Pole there was great joy, mixed with relief. Everyone was thankful for another blessed year. Papa, along with the others, arrived to find everyone outside to greet them with great news.

Not only had the town folk repaired the barn door, putting it back on its hinges – but also they had spent Christmas day together repairing many of the roofs that had collapsed. Some were able to go back to their homes and were sharing them with neighbors until all could be fixed. The elves had been great hosts, they said, but the ceilings were "most certainly" a little low, they chuckled.

By dinnertime the "Snowed-Out Santas'" families had arrived and were heartily welcomed. Dinner had been prepared and Papa's home was overflowing with white haired, white bearded men and their families, along with one glowing white-haired young lady, all hungry and ready to eat.

"Brothers, please come with your wives and families to the Hall of North Pole Santas, where we will offer thanksgiving for another

The Legend of the Twenty-First North Pole Santa

blessed year for the Santa Claus family – and then we will eat," he added with a Santa laugh that only Papa had.

As the Twentieth North Pole Santa, Papa gave the blessing beneath the portrait of the first North Pole Santa, saying, "I give thanks for the blessings and new understandings that have been given this year. We are blessed with family that reaches not only around the world but into the heart. We are blessed with neighbors, including our friends the elves, who shared their homes at a time of need. We are blessed with a history and heritage going back to the first North Pole Santa, who started our traditions with his wife and sons."

Then, as Papa was ready to continue, he was suddenly interrupted. Hearing that someone had started to speak, Papa was startled and looked up toward the voice, which continued without the drop of a beat. "And we are thankful for the new traditions, like those started here tonight – when a Little Star helped guide our way – and with my son's permission — will begin a new tradition as the Twenty-First North Pole Santa.

Nicky's enthusiasm was uncontrollable. It's what he had wanted all along. He just needed his father to realize that it was right. Leaping into the air, Nicky let loose with a "Merry Christmas! Merry Christmas, Holly!" and reached for Holly, who had been standing by his side and swung her around till she was nearly delirious with dizziness and Nicky had to be stopped.

Gaining his breath and composure, Nicky then allowed his father to continue and Holly to see straight again. Turning to his son, he said, "I take it, then, that I have your permission, Nickolai." Slightly embarrassed, Nicky laughed, along with everyone else.

Holly, still a little dizzy, walked to her uncle and said, "Thank you uncle. This means so much to Papa, Mama and me, and I know that my birth parents are smiling down on us tonight, as well."

Looking out at her many uncles, aunts and cousins, Holly reflected, "We come from a diverse family, with wonderful traditions going back to First North Pole Santa and Papa and Mama taught me that traditions are to be respected." Then she paused for an instant and quickly added, "But I am so glad that there is room for new traditions!" Everyone broke into a cheer then, while Mama and Papa looked at each other, then at Uncle Noel, who gave them a wink.

Chapter XIV Christmas is Over

Denise Graham Zahn

The Legend of the Twenty-First North Pole Santa

After dinner an open house was held. Friends and neighbors, including the elves, stopped in to share another joyous Christmas in the home of Papa and his family. And when Holly went out to say good night to Rudy and the other reindeer, someone remarked that they saw what appeared to be a little star glowing in the barn.

Papa just looked at Mama and smiled.

Epilogue

It may seem that this is the end of the story, but it isn't. The magic of Christmas continued into the next year, as girls were born into the Santa Claus family for the first time ever. Seven years after her initiation, a married Holly gave birth to a son, whom they named Ely. Ely had a special gift that showed itself as he grew older. Like his Grandfather Papa, he was a great storyteller—better than his sister and all of his cousins—but not quite as good as Grandfather, "at least not yet," Papa always declared.

Holly's daughter was called Little Star, for like her mother, she had a magic of her own that people spoke of when at night she could be seen as clearly as a star in the distant sky. Her glow came from within, but it magically spread to everyone around her.

Yes. Like the Believing World, the Santa Claus family grew and spread out in all directions. They follow many treasured traditions, but now and then add a new one or two. So the story never ends, you see. Just like the spirit of Christmas, it goes on and on and on…

About the Author

Denise Graham Zahn, of Chicago, earned a master's degree in Media Communications from Governors State University, completing a thesis titled, *American Indians – Taking Technology Road to the Twenty-First Century*.

She has written freelance features for regional newspapers; wrote and produced a one-act play at Prairie State College; has a poem published in *The American Poetry Anthology*; was editor of the Governors State University student newspaper, and worked as Coordinator of Public Information for Governors State University, writing stories and press releases for print publications.

She is married and has two children and two granddaughters, along with two dogs (rescued greyhound and Italian greyhound), a cat and two parakeets.

The Legend of the Twenty-First North Pole Santa is her first published book.

Printed in the United Kingdom
by Lightning Source UK Ltd.
103464UKS00002B/177